ROOM
for Rent

Leah Goldberg

Illustrations by Shmuel Katz
Translated from the Hebrew by Jessica Setbon

Layout: Optume Technologies
Editing: Lisa Sanders

Published by arrangement with the Institute for the Translation of Hebrew Literature

ISBN: 978-965-229-920-8

1 3 5 7 9 8 6 4 2

Gefen Publishing House Ltd.
6 Hatzvi Street
Jerusalem 9438614, Israel
972-2-538-0247
orders@gefenpublishing.com

www.gefenpublishing.com
Printed in Israel
2018/5778

Library of Congress Cataloging-in-Publication Data

Names: Goldberg, Leah, 1911-1970, author. | Katz, Shmuel, 1926-2010,
illustrator. | Setbon, Jessica, translator.
Title: Room for rent / by Leah Goldberg ; illustrations by Shmuel Katz ;
translated from the Hebrew by Jessica Setbon.
Other titles: Dira Lehaskir. English
Description: Springfield, NJ : Gefen Books, [2017] | Summary: The diverse
residents of an apartment house get along fine, but when they try to rent
a vacant room, each prospective tenant finds fault with one of them.
Identifiers: LCCN 2017032342 | ISBN 9789652299208
Subjects: | CYAC: Stories in rhyme. | Neighbors--Fiction. | Apartment
houses--Fiction. | Toleration--Fiction. | Animals--Fiction.
Classification: LCC PZ8.3.G565 Ro 2017 | DDC [Fic]--dc23 LC record available at
https://lccn.loc.gov/2017032342

Room for Rent

5th Floor
Sir Reginald Mouse

4th Floor
Squirrel

3rd Floor
Mrs. Cat

2nd Floor
Cuckoo Bird

1st Floor
Miss Hen

In a sunlit valley, 'tween meadow and sky,
Stands a fine old house that's five stories high.

On the first floor is a Cornish hen, heavy and stout.
All day long she lazes about.
Our friend Miss Hen is so fat and coddled,
She can barely manage a walk or a waddle.

On the second floor lives a Cuckoo bird.
Her chicks are all scattered, you may have heard.
From dawn to dusk she makes her rounds
To visit her children in other towns.

On the third floor is a Cat who's finicky clean.
She combs her whiskers, so pristine.
With fur that's darkest midnight black
And a bow round her neck – she's vain about that.

On the fourth floor lives a tranquil Squirrel,
With her friends she's never picked a quarrel.
She cracks pecans to her heart's content,
And says, "This peace is heaven sent."

Up on floor five lived Sir Reginald Mouse,
Until one week ago, when he left the house,
And to this day, we have our doubts
That anyone knows his whereabouts.

The committee got together and drew up a sign
In large block letters, in one straight line.
They hung the sign on a nail on the door.
It read "Room for Rent," not one word more.

By highway and byway, past hills and down dales.
New tenants came knocking, telling their tales.

First was Miss Ant. She marched up to floor five,
Opened the door and peeked inside.
The neighbors all gathered around to spy
As Miss Ant checked the place with a critical eye.
They asked her, politely, if the rooms were alright.
Perhaps she would like to stay for the night?

Are the rooms nice?
          Yes, they'll suffice.
Will the kitchen do?
          It's just right, too.
Do you like the hall?
          It's fine, that's all.
So come live with us, Miss Ant!
          I can't.
Why not?

The Ant replied in a nasty gripe:
"Sorry, but the neighbors are not my type.
A hard-working Ant can hardly reside
With a lazy Hen whom she cannot abide.
The Miss Hen in this house is so fat and coddled,
She can hardly manage a walk or a waddle!"

The Hen was hurt and turned her back.
Miss Ant went away, no need to unpack.

As soon as she'd gone, in bounded Mrs. Rabbit.
She bounced up the stairs, as was her habit.
She read the sign and took a long look.
Her soft, furry ears quivered and shook.

The neighbors all gathered around to spy
As the Rabbit checked the place with a critical eye.
They asked her, politely, if the rooms were alright.
Perhaps she would like to stay for the night?

Are the rooms nice?
        Yes, they'll suffice.
Will the kitchen do?
        It's just right, too.
Do you like the hall?
        It's fine, that's all.
So Mrs. Rabbit, please stay.
        No way!

"I'm sorry," she gasped, "but to make it short,
The neighbors are simply not the right sort.
How can a mother with twenty young ones
Live with a Cuckoo who abandons her sons?
The Cuckoo's chicks sleep in other moms' nests;
She abandons each one, along with the rest.
What kind of example is she for my brood?
Don't beg me to stay, I'm not in the mood!"

The Cuckoo bird stalked out in a huff.
Mrs. Rabbit raced off, she'd had more than enough.

With Mrs. Rabbit gone, in came Snortimus Pig
In a porkpie hat and a curly wig.
He read the sign, "Room for Rent,"
Tumbled inside and up he went.
His tiny eyes peered at the ceiling and floor,
The windows and walls, while he stood at the door.

The neighbors all gathered around to spy
As the Pig scanned the place with a critical eye.
They asked him, politely, if the rooms were alright.
Perhaps he would like to stay for the night?

Are the rooms nice?
          Yes, they'll suffice.
And the kitchen, what do you say?
          Far too clean, but okay.
Do you like our hall?
          It's fine, that's all.
Then Snortimus, will you remain?
          Heavens, no! I must complain!

"The neighbors are not to my taste, I'm afraid.
There's been a huge error, a mistake has been made.
Me, in the same house as a Cat with black fur?
A white thoroughbred Pig cannot live next to her."

The neighbors did not remain silent for long.
"Get out of here, Pig!" they cried. "Scoot! Run along!
You're the mistake, you're the one who's all wrong!"

Room for
Rent

"Goodbye!" grunted Snortimus, tossing his tail.
Then in waltzed a honey-voiced Nightingale.

The Nightingale sang a melodious song,
As she flew up the staircase, it didn't take long.
She read the sign and opened the door,
Examined the walls, the ceiling, the floor.

The neighbors all gathered around to spy
As the Nightingale gazed with a critical eye.
They asked her, politely, if the rooms were alright.
Perhaps she would like to stay for the night?

Are the rooms nice?
        Yes, they'll suffice.
And the kitchen will do?
        It's just right, too.
Then stay with us, please!

"No, I won't stay or ask for the keys.
The neighbors are dreadful, as everyone sees.
How can I enjoy my peace and quiet
When that Squirrel downstairs is creating a riot?
She cracks those nuts the whole day through;
The noise is worse than in a zoo!
My delicate ears need a beautiful tune,
Not a squirrelsome racket that makes me swoon."

The Squirrel flinched and took offense.
The Nightingale flew off over the fence.

With the nightingale gone, in floated the Dove.
She flitted and fluttered to the top floor above.
She read the sign and opened the door,
Examined the walls, the ceiling, the floor.

The neighbors all gathered around to spy
As the Dove glanced about with a critical eye.
They asked her, politely, if the rooms were alright.
Perhaps she would like to stay for the night?

    Are the rooms nice?
        They're small, at this price.
    Will the kitchen do?
        It's narrow, that's true.
    The hallway, is it roomy?
        It's dark and gloomy.
    So you won't stay with us?
        "Yes, I will!" cooed the Dove.
        "And in fact, I would love
        To live here among you."

"Miss Hen, I can see, is a feathery friend.
This sweet Cuckoo bird is true to her word.
The cat's so pristine, not a speck can be seen.
The Squirrel shares her treasured nuts –
A generous neighbor, no ifs, ands or buts.
I'm sure we'll be able to get along.
Our friendly ties will remain steady and strong."

The Dove decided to rent the room.
Now she sits at her window and grooms her plume.

In a sunlit valley, 'tween meadow and sky,
Stands a fine old house that's five stories high.
With laughter that rings from every floor,
True friends and good neighbors, who could ask
for more?